Bookworm Library

Written by Sarah Toast
Illustrated by Elena Kucharik

Copyright © 1996 Publications International, Ltd.

ISBN: 0-7853-1934-4

Leap Frog is a trademark of Publications International, Ltd.

Cora Caterpillar is the librarian at the Bookworm Library. She takes care of the library and all of the books inside.

The Bookworm Library has books about all sorts of things. The young bugs love to read about exciting places and fun things to do.

Cora reminds the bug children to stay quiet in the library. It makes it easier for the grown-up bugs to read.

Story hour is Cora's favorite time of the day. She loves reading storybooks to the youngest bugs in Bugtown.

After story hour the bug kids look for books to take home. Wally Waterbug finds a book about boats. Sally Spider picks a book about weaving.

When each bug child has found a book, they go downstairs to check out. After Cora stamps the books, the bug children can read them at home for two whole weeks.

The young bugs take their books and head for home. But where is Rollie Roly-Poly? Cora knows just where to find him.

Cora wakes up Rollie and sends him home. She loves being a librarian and helping out the young bugs in Bugtown.